Even Higher

For Levi Cohen Chatinover
B. C.

For Barbara
A. I.

First Edition   1 2 3 4 5 6 7 8 9 10

Library of Congress Cataloging in Publication Data   Cohen, Barbara.   Even higher. Adaptation of: Oyb nisht nokh hekher, by I. L. Peretz. Summary: A skeptical visitor to the village of Nemirov finds out where its rabbi really goes during the Jewish New Year, when the villagers claim he goes to heaven to speak to God. [1. Folklore, Jewish] I. Ivanov, Anatoly, ill. II. Peretz, Isaac Leib, 1851 or 2-1915. Oyb nisht nokh hekher. III. Title.   PZ8.1.C6644Ev   1987   398.2′089924   [E]   86-7419 ISBN 0-688-06452-3   ISBN 0-688-06453-1 (lib. bdg.)

Even Higher

BY BARBARA COHEN
RETOLD FROM THE STORY BY I. L. PERETZ

Illustrated by Anatoly Ivanov

LOTHROP, LEE & SHEPARD BOOKS   NEW YORK

Some people don't believe what they're told. They believe only what they see. Missourians are said to be like that. That's why Missouri is called the "Show Me" State.

Lithuania is a long way from Missouri. But they used to say that people from Lithuania were doubters too. They called those people Litvaks.

One bright September day, a Litvak arrived in a little Ukrainian town called Nemirov. It was right before Rosh Hashanah, the Jewish New Year, the birthday of the world.

In the marketplace people noticed the Litvak. A stranger stood out in Nemirov.

"Welcome to our town," said the Grain Merchant.

"Thank you," said the Litvak.

"I think I know why you came right before the New Year."

"Do you?" the Litvak asked, raising one eyebrow.

"We get up very early every morning in the weeks before the New Year to say the special prayers asking God's forgiveness for our sins—" the Grain Merchant began.

"What Jew doesn't?" interrupted the Litvak. "We all want to be as pure as new babies for the birthday of the world."

The Fishmonger had been listening. "Let him finish," she scolded.

The Litvak raised his other eyebrow. "Go ahead, finish."

"At this holy time of the year you have come to see our Rabbi," said the Grain Merchant.

"Why would I want to see your Rabbi?" asked the Litvak.

It was the Horse Trader who answered. "Our Rabbi is the holiest man in the world. The holiest man in the universe."

The Litvak smiled. "Every town thinks its Rabbi is the holiest."

"But ours really is," said the Fishmonger.

"Please," said the Litvak, "don't tell me any fairy stories."

The Horse Trader went on as if he hadn't heard. "On Fridays during the New Year season, our Rabbi disappears very early in the morning. You can't find him anywhere. Not in his house or in anyone else's. Not at prayers. Not on the streets. Not anywhere."

The Litvak laughed.

"It's true," the Fishmonger insisted. "But we know where he goes."

The Litvak's lip curled. "Do you?"

The Fishmonger nodded. "He raises himself right up to Heaven. He stands in front of God and with his own mouth asks Him to forgive the poor, sinful people of Nemirov."

The Litvak snorted.

"God admits our Rabbi into His presence," the Fishmonger snapped. "What more proof do you need that our Rabbi is the holiest man living?"

"Your Rabbi doesn't rise up to Heaven," declared the Litvak. "Even Moses had to wait until he was dead to get to Heaven."

"Then where does our Rabbi go?" asked the Grain Merchant.

"I don't know," the Litvak retorted. "And I don't care."

But he made up his mind to find out.

That very evening, while the Rabbi was at prayers, the Litvak sneaked into the Rabbi's house. The Rabbi's door wasn't locked. Who would steal from the holy Rabbi of Nemirov?

The Litvak hid under the Rabbi's bed. After a while the Rabbi came in, undressed, climbed into bed, and fell asleep.

Another man would have dozed off, but not the Litvak. He kept himself awake all night reciting in his head whole chapters from the Bible.

It was still dark when the house woke up. The Litvak could hear the sounds of beds squeaking. He could hear footsteps, voices, and splashing water. Then the house was silent again. Everyone had left for the special New Year prayers. Everyone—except the Rabbi and the Litvak.

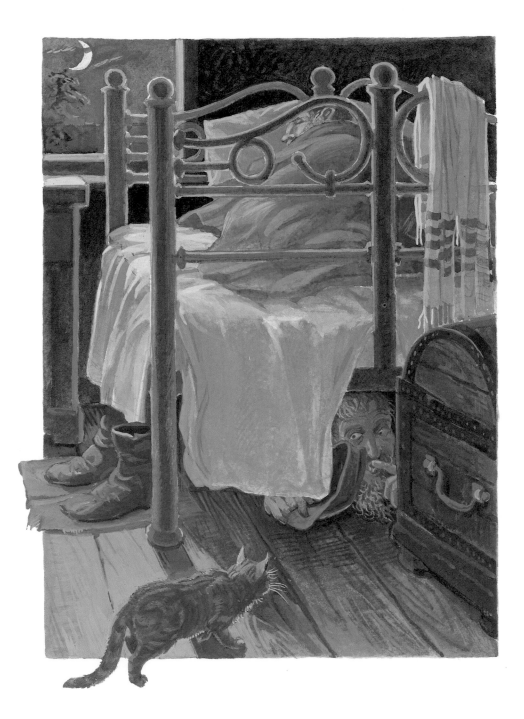

Now it was the Rabbi's turn to get up. From under the bed, the Litvak watched. The Rabbi didn't take his usual black coat, white stockings, and fur hat out of the wardrobe. Instead he put on linen trousers, tall boots, a coarse smock, a cap, and a wide belt studded with nails. He looked like a common peasant. A rope dangled from the pocket of the smock.

The Rabbi left the bedroom. On tiptoes and crouching, ducking behind doors and tables, the Litvak followed. An ax hung on the kitchen wall. The Rabbi slipped it through his belt and left the house.

The Litvak followed the Rabbi of Nemirov through the dim, hushed town. Avoiding the main streets, they kept to the shadows cast by narrow houses. Then the buildings grew farther and farther apart, until finally there were no more. The Litvak found himself in the forest beyond the town.

Now he hid behind a bush. He watched while the Rabbi took his ax and struck a tree. The Rabbi, a scholar and a holy man, cutting down a tree, like a peasant! The Litvak had never seen such a thing. Chop, chop, chop. The tree fell. The Rabbi split the trunk into logs and the logs into sticks. He tied the sticks together with his rope, slung the whole bundle over his shoulder, and returned to town.

The Litvak followed, wondering.

On the poorest street stood a tiny hut. The holes in the single window were stuffed with rags. The door hung half on, half off its rusted hinges. The Rabbi knocked.

"Who's there?" called a weak, frightened voice.

"Me," answered the Rabbi.

"Who's me?"

"Vassily."

"Which Vassily?" the voice whined. "So many are named Vassily. What do you want?"

"I'm Vassily the woodchopper," said the Rabbi. "I have wood to sell. Very cheap, next to nothing." And he entered the hut.

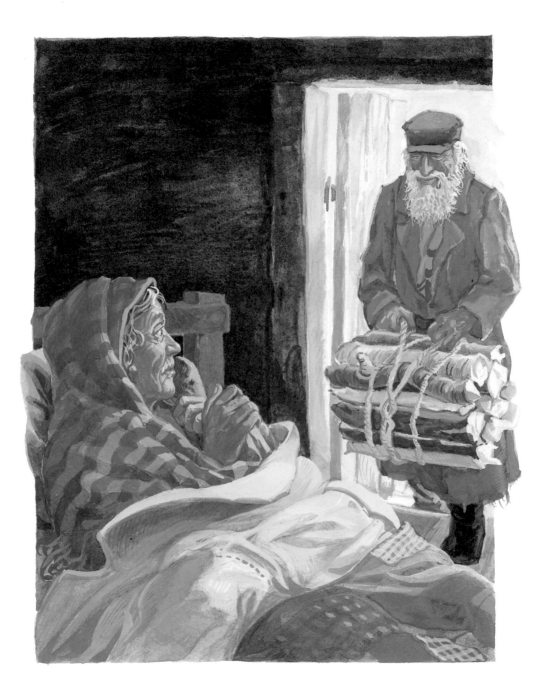

The Litvak peered in through the window. He saw a small room furnished with only a bed, a wooden table, and a stool. No fire burned in the stove. A skinny old woman lay coughing and shivering under a pile of rags. "Wood?" she said. "Where am I, a poor sick widow, going to get the money to buy wood?"

"You don't have to pay me now," said the Rabbi. "I'll give it to you on credit."

"Where will I *ever* get the money to pay you?" she complained.

"I'm willing to trust you," said the Rabbi. "Can't you trust God?"

"So, then, who's to light the fire?" She groaned. "Do I look as if I can do it?"

The Rabbi laid some wood in the stove and murmured
one of the special New Year prayers. He lit the fire and
murmured another prayer. He piled the rest of the wood
in a corner and murmured a third prayer.

The Litvak saw and heard it all. His mouth dropped
open in astonishment.

The Litvak remained in Nemirov forever after, one of the Rabbi's most faithful followers.

And when the Grain Merchant or the Fishmonger or anyone else in the town would tell a stranger how their Rabbi, right before the New Year, raised himself to Heaven, the Litvak would smile.

And then he would add quietly:

"Even higher."

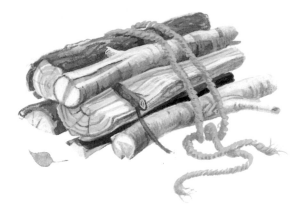

ACKNOWLEDGMENT

"*Oib Nisht Noch Hecher*" by Isaac Loeb Peretz (1852–1915) has often been translated from the original Yiddish into English, occasionally under the title "Even Higher," more often as "If Not Higher." My version is not a translation, but an adaptation.

I did not adapt the story because I thought I could improve upon the efforts of a master like Peretz. That would be impossible. I adapted it in the hope of making it more accessible than the original to contemporary American children of all creeds. Peretz was steeped in Hassidic lore and tradition. His version too is in some sense a retelling. Since his text is the one that has come down to us, we cannot know the exact extent to which the power of his genius shaped, enriched, and elevated his sources.

—B.C.